*This is the story of two brave Dalmatians, ninety-nine puppies,
and one of the greatest rescues of all time.*

Pongo and Perdita lived in London with their people pets, Roger and Anita.

When Perdita and Pongo became parents of fifteen little puppies, they were so proud!

Life seemed perfect… until an old friend of Anita's—Cruella De Vil!—came to see the puppies.

Cruella waltzed into the room demanding to see the adorable puppies and their beautiful coats. She even proclaimed that she would buy them all.

"We're not selling the puppies," said Roger. "Not a single one."

"You fools!" Cruella cried. "You'll be sorry!" And she stormed out of the house.

One night, Cruella sent her two henchmen, the
Badun Brothers, to dognap the puppies!
The police immediately launched an investigation,
but as the days went by, the puppies were still not found.

At last, Pongo said to Perdita, "I'm afraid it's all up to us."

Pongo decided to try the Twilight Bark. This was the quickest way for dogs to send and receive news across the country.

That evening, from the top of Primrose Hill, Pongo sent the alarm:

"Bark, bark, bark, h-o-w-l!"

Then Pongo and Perdita waited.

After a moment, an answering bark was heard.

"It's the Great Dane at Hampstead!" said Pongo, and he barked the message about the missing puppies.

The Great Dane then barked out an all-dog alert, sending the news all over London.

The Twilight Bark reached an old sheepdog called the Colonel, who lived on a farm. The Colonel's friends—a horse named the Captain and a cat named Sergeant Tibs—listened, too. They were all concerned to hear that fifteen puppies had been stolen.

"That's funny," Tibs said to the Captain and the Colonel. "I heard puppies barking over at the old De Vil house last night."

"No one's lived there for years!" said the Colonel. "We must go and see what's going on."

So the Colonel and Tibs went quietly up to the house and peered through a broken window.

Inside the house, Horace and Jasper Badun were eating supper and relaxing in front of the television.

All around the room there were puppies.
Not fifteen puppies.
Not even fifty puppies.
Tibs counted *ninety-nine* puppies!

The Colonel quickly returned to the Captain's stable and loudly barked the good news. Within no time at all, the Twilight Bark sent the message all the way back to London that the puppies had been found.

The good news finally reached the ears of Perdita and Pongo. They set off across the snowy countryside as fast as they could to rescue their puppies.

Meanwhile, Sergeant Tibs was keeping watch on the house. He peeked in and saw Cruella barking out orders. She wanted the puppies' skins for coats. "I'll be back first thing in the morning!"

Fur coats! How awful!

Tibs could not believe it.

He had to save these poor puppies!

There wasn't a moment to lose. As soon as the Baduns began watching television again, Tibs crept through the broken window and whispered, "Hey, kids! You'd better get out of here if you want to save your skins!"

When all the puppies had been alerted, Tibs led them out of the room and up the stairs to find a hiding place.

Meanwhile, the Colonel had met up with Perdita and Pongo and led them to the De Vil house. They arrived just in the nick of time and quickly bounded into action.

Perdita went after Horace, while Pongo tore at Jasper Badun's trousers.

As the fight was going on, Sergeant Tibs led the puppies out of the house to the safety of the Captain's stable.

Leaving the Baduns in a heap, Perdita and Pongo dashed after the puppies. When they got to the barn, Perdita checked to see if her fifteen puppies were there.

"Your fifteen and a few more," replied the Captain. "There are *ninety-nine!*"

"*Ninety-nine!*" said Pongo, astonished. "Whatever did Cruella want with *ninety-nine* puppies?"

There was silence for a moment, then one little
puppy said, "She was going to make coats out of us."
    Perdita and Pongo looked at each other in horror.
They had never heard of anything so evil.
    "We'll take them home with us," said Pongo.
He was sure Roger and Anita would look after them.

Perdita, Pongo, and the
puppies set off back to London.
Fearing that Cruella would come
after them, Pongo made the puppies
roll in some soot until they all looked
like black Labradors.

"Quick! Into this van!" said Pongo.
"It's going to London!"

Pongo had just enough time to leap onto the tailboard as the van sped off—escaping Cruella and the Baduns!

Back in London and home at last, Roger and Anita hugged the tired puppies.

"Fourteen, fifteen," counted Roger, "sixty-two—ninety-four—and five over there. That's a hundred and one Dalmatians, counting Perdita and Pongo!"

"What'll we do with them?" asked Anita.

"We'll keep them," said Roger. "We'll have a plantation! A Dalmatian plantation!" And that's exactly what they did!